The Secret Time Machine and the Gherkin Switcheroo

The Secret Time Machine and the Gherkin Switcheroo

Simone Lia

Copyright © 2019 by Simone Lia

First U.S. edition 2020

Library of Congress Catalog Card Number pending
ISBN 978-1-5362-0740-8

20 21 22 23 24 25 APS 10 9 8 7 6 5 4 3 2 1

Printed in Humen, Dongguan, China

This book was typeset in Veronan and WB Simonelia.
The illustrations were done in mixed media.

Candlewick Press
99 Dover Street
Somerville, Massachusetts 02144

visit us at www.candlewick.com

A JUNIOR LIBRARY GUILD SELECTION

For my darling AJ

Chapter One

It's me, Marcus.

I don't mean to be rude, but have we met before? In case we haven't, let me tell you a little bit about myself. My name is Marcus, and I'm a worm.

As far as worms go, I'm quite ordinary. I love digging holes in the mud, wriggling, eating, beatboxing, and dreaming about potatoes. Most of these hobbies are not *that* unusual.

Laurence

Me

One of the things about me that is different is that I don't live in the ground. I live in a house in a tree with a big, fat bird named Laurence.

Laurence is my best friend. I don't know many other worms who live in a birdhouse. Actually, I know exactly zero worms who live in a birdhouse.

To be honest with you, I wasn't too sure about Laurence when I first met him.

Are you going to eat me for breakfast?

3

The day we met he *insisted* I travel with him on an epic journey to Kenya. I didn't really want to go, but flying to a distant land with a bird who looked like a chicken was a lot better than being eaten by one.

It was only after having a long and adventurous journey that I got to know him.

Neither of us expected to become such excellent friends. I ended up moving into his house so that we could be together every single day. At first, everything was great. We'd have picnics near the highway or we'd wear butterfly costumes or we'd

4

pretend to be robots that had malfunctioned and spend the whole day talking backward.

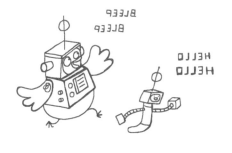

No two days were ever the same. But when Laurence discovered a new and very boring hobby, he didn't want to do anything interesting anymore. He didn't even want to leave the house. These days, he sits on the sofa every waking hour like a great big blob of mashed potatoes with his new favorite thing: crossword puzzle books. It's SO boring!

Since he became a crossword puzzle fanatic, EVERYTHING has changed. . . .

Chapter Two

Laurence was sitting in his favorite spot with his head buried in his book. He had cookie crumbs in his feathers, and his beak was crusty from yesterday's French onion soup.

"I'm stuck on a clue," he moaned. He was *always* stuck on a clue.

"Read it aloud," I sighed.

"*Farm animal.* Three letters, beginning with *P.*"

"*Pig.*"

"You're so good at crosswords, Marcus!" he cheered as he wrote the letters carefully in the boxes.

"I'm much better at digging!" I shot back. "Can we go outside and make a tunnel?"

"No, thanks," he said politely. "It's raining. Let's have a stay-at-home day today."

"Aw! We stay at home *every* day. It's been FOREVER since we've gone out and had any fun. You *never* want to do anything I want these days."

He put his pen down in a huff. "That's not fair. I'm a bird, and birds don't like being underground. How would *you* feel if I made you do something that worms don't like doing?"

You made me fly to Kenya with you.

I whispered in a small voice without moving my lips.

7

"I heard that, Marcus. That was completely different. We didn't even really know each other then. Here's another clue," he said, changing the subject back to crosswords.

"I'm not telling you the answer until you agree to go outside."

Laurence looked worried. He half closed his book. "Do you want to do this puzzle instead?" He held up a box with a picture of a dog carrying a basket of kittens and flowers.

"No," I said grumpily, even though it looked really fun. "I want to play outside."

Laurence closed his eyes to think for a moment. "How about if you go out to play and I watch you from up here? I'll be able to see you if I lean out of the window."

I shook my head. "It's not the same."

He sighed heavily. "OK, I'll come with you."

8

Even though he didn't seem excited by the idea, this was the first time he'd agreed to leave the birdhouse in ages.

"I'll need to wear a special outfit, though, so I won't get mud on my feathers," he added. He waited a few seconds before saying, "Too bad we don't have anything suitable in the dresser. We'll just have to stay home instead."

I flopped down from my chair. He wasn't going to wriggle out of it that easily. "*I'll* MAKE something for you, Laurence. I just need trash bags, tape, and a jar of gherkins."

"What do you need the jar of gherkins for?"

"To eat while I'm working on your outfit."

"Fine," Laurence grumbled. "I'll get the things you need." He stood up slowly. A piece of cheese sandwich that had been tucked in his feathers fell to the floor. He dragged his feet in slow motion toward one of the cupboards.

I felt annoyed and sorry for Laurence at the same time. "We don't *have* to go outside if you don't want to," I said without thinking.

"Oh, all right then," he chirped, dropping the roll of trash bags on the floor and hopping back to the sofa at great speed.

I was mad at myself for speaking without thinking. Sometimes I wished I had a special machine that PLONK would let me undo the stupid things I'd just said. Like a time machine. If I had one of those, I'd use it a lot!

Laurence read another clue: "*Fruit from a tree, five letters, second letter P.*"

"*Apple.*" I sighed.

He wrote the letters in the boxes, whistling from his beak as he breathed. I could feel my blood pressure rising.

Why couldn't he breathe like a normal bird?

10

I wondered what it would be like to have an actual time machine. There would be so much we could do with it! I'd definitely use it to stop Laurence from taking up crosswords as a hobby. And then we could go back eighty million years dressed as robots. *That* would totally confuse the dinosaurs!

coo-eee

Laurence interrupted my thoughts as he loudly snorted to clear his nasal beak passages. Did he really have to make such horrible noises ALL the time? He was always clearing his beak or whistle-breathing or stirring his mug of hot chocolate and making a *clink-clink-clinkity-clink* sound. It was SO annoying.

Klaghem, clag, clag, clag, aghem!

CLINK-CLINK-CLINK

11

Also, since he'd adopted the habit of being boring and lazy and sitting on the sofa all day, he'd stopped taking his regular bird baths and now he smelled like a sweaty goat. No offense to goats.

I shook my head; I'd had just about enough of Laurence with his disgusting smells and irritating noises!

"What are you thinking about?" Laurence asked cheerfully as he stirred a mug of hot chocolate, making a *clink-clink-clinkity-clink* sound.

"NOTHING," I answered abruptly. I couldn't tell him what I was thinking; it was too horrible.

"It looked as though you were deep in thought."

"I was thinking about a time machine," I said in a panic.

"What time machine?"

I blurted out the first thing that came into my head: "The one that my auntie built."

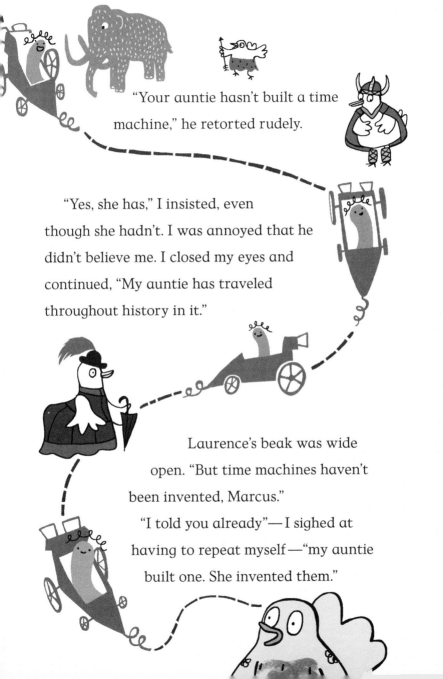

"Your auntie hasn't built a time machine," he retorted rudely.

"Yes, she has," I insisted, even though she hadn't. I was annoyed that he didn't believe me. I closed my eyes and continued, "My auntie has traveled throughout history in it."

Laurence's beak was wide open. "But time machines haven't been invented, Marcus."

"I told you already"—I sighed at having to repeat myself—"my auntie built one. She invented them."

He sat up straight on the sofa. "Has she really?"

I nodded, smiling proudly. "She certainly did." I was excellent at lying.

"Can we go see it and travel into the past?"

I hadn't thought that far ahead, so I sat there like a worm statue, thinking of what to say.

"Are you OK, Marcus? You look funny."

"Yes, I'm fine; I was just thinking about what we might eat for dinner."

"Can we go see it?" Laurence asked again.

"Definitely, yes." I didn't know what else to say.

Laurence stood up and clapped his wings above his head while wiggling his hips. The rest of his cheese sandwich fell from his armpit onto the floor. It smelled like it had been in there for years.

14

"I'm going to take a bath to celebrate."

"At last!" I cheered joyfully.

Laurence looked upset.

"I mean, at last . . . you'll get to see my auntie's invention. You're going to love it."

"I will!" He hopped to the bathroom. "I can't believe you didn't mention this before! We can go as soon as it stops raining."

"I can't wait!" I called out.

At last, we were going to leave the birdhouse and breathe some fresh air. I wish I'd lied about my auntie having a time machine weeks ago.

I lay down on the floor and looked at the ceiling and made a mental list of all the things I needed to do before we left the house. I just needed to:

A - Find out how time travel works.

B - Build a time machine without Laurence noticing.

C - Do A and B before it stopped raining.

It probably wouldn't be too difficult to do all of that. . . .

ticktock
ticktock
ticktock

Chapter Three

Building a time machine was going to be a lot harder than I'd first imagined. Even though Laurence had been taking the world's longest bath, I hadn't had a single idea how to do it. I didn't even understand how time travel worked. I was pretty sure they hadn't taught us *that* at worm school.

A panicky feeling rose through my worm body. I needed to invent something before it stopped raining. The sun loomed behind a rain cloud; it could beam its way out at any moment and ruin everything.

I paced backward and forward; it was hard to concentrate with the grandfather clock ticking so loudly. Even wearing Laurence's socks on my head did nothing to muffle the *ticktock*ing. Everything was going wrong!

18

"Are you all right?"
Laurence asked suspiciously.

"I'm completely fine,"
I said, shaking off my
ear socks. He blew his
beak noisily with a
handkerchief and hopped
into the bedroom.

I circled the room at great speed, hoping it
might get my brain juices flowing.

It didn't work.

*Maybe I'll have an idea if I sit somewhere
different,* I thought.

"Are you *sure* you're all
right?" It was Laurence
again. He looked worried.

I tried to convince him. "Yes, I feel exactly the same as I felt a minute ago. Never better."

"Oh . . . OK then," he replied before shuffling into the kitchen.

As soon as his back was turned, I frantically swung around and around while hanging from the lampshade to activate my worm brain. And then it happened: a brilliant idea popped into my head.

Laurence had a huge collection of books. He would DEFINITELY have something in his library that explained how to build a time machine. I dropped and rolled to the shelves with glee. There were books on history, travel, learning German, knitting, steamrollers, science, tree house design, cake baking, advanced electromagnetic field theory, and quilting, to name just a few. But I couldn't find any books about time machines.

I was about to start panicking again, when I wondered what kind of books a very smart inventor-type person would read if they wanted to build a time machine.

"Probably science books," I said out loud by accident.

"What are you doing?" Laurence asked as he came back out of the kitchen. He had a sandwich and four chocolate snack cakes piled on his plate.

"I'm choosing a book to read."

Laurence looked very, very concerned now. "But you don't like reading."

I ignored him and pulled out a large book on quilt making. "This one looks good." I didn't want him to guess that I was doing research for my invention.

"Are you totally and utterly sure you're feeling OK? I can get the thermometer and take your temperature if you want."

Laurence asking me how I was feeling every five minutes was making me hot and sweaty. Maybe I *wasn't* fine, after all.

"I've never felt better," I lied. "I'm going to sit quietly and read this. I've always wanted to learn how to sew a patchwork quilt."

"All right, then." He seemed to believe me.

As he hopped to the sofa, I sneaked a science book into *Quilt Making for Beginners* and flicked through the pages.

 There was a chapter on something called quantum physics that explained time travel.

EINSTEIN'S THEORY OF RELATIVITY

← Albert Einstein

THE math · · ·

$$R_{\mu\nu} - \tfrac{1}{2} R g_{\mu\nu} + \Lambda g_{\mu\nu} = \tfrac{8\pi G}{c^4} T_{\mu\nu}$$

or

$$G_{\mu\nu} = R_{\mu\nu} - \tfrac{1}{2} R g_{\mu\nu}$$

and then...

"I'm going to learn everything there is to learn about quantum physics," I muttered with joy. Fortunately, Laurence was too busy eating his sandwich to hear me.

It said that for time travel to be possible, you needed to move faster than the speed of light. This could be a problem. I only had a bicycle, and I didn't think it would be able to go *that* fast, even with Laurence pedaling down the huge hill near our house.

Then something caught my eye. There was a part about a scientist named Albert Einstein, who a long time ago said that time travel could be possible through a thing called a "wormhole." I couldn't believe it! I'm a worm: I dig holes!

My kind of wormhole

Ta-da!

The wormhole in the book

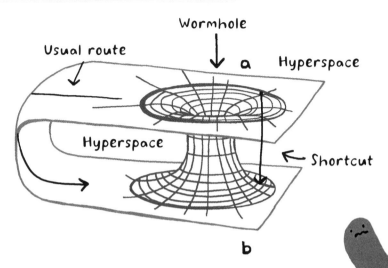

Wormhole

Usual route

Hyperspace

a

Hyperspace

Shortcut

b

The wormholes in the picture didn't look anything like the holes I dig, though. They were in outer space. How would I get *there* on my bike? As I continued, I read that scientists didn't even know whether wormholes existed.

What's the point of that then?

I grumbled out loud.

"What did you say, Marcus?" Laurence's face was smeared with blobs of mayonnaise from his sandwich.

"Oh, um, I was saying that this quilt has very delicate needlepoint."

Laurence didn't reply. I felt angry with Albert Einstein for being so smart. I slammed the book shut. I was *really* angry with Laurence, too. If it wasn't for him not wanting to play outside with me, I wouldn't have to trick him into leaving the house by going to the trouble of inventing and building a time machine.

SLAM

It was all too much. I didn't want to be an inventor anymore. I wanted to do something that *I* enjoyed and that *I* knew how to do.

I've had enough!

Of reading about quilts?

"No. Of EVERYTHING. I'm going to play in the mud all by myself."

Laurence looked taken aback. "But it's raining."

"I LIKE the rain!" I shouted as I wriggled across the floor. I wanted to swing the front door wide open to make a dramatic exit, but I couldn't reach the handle. So Laurence had to come and open it for me.

He poked his head out to speak to me on the porch. "Would you like me to give you a lift to the bottom of the tree?"

"Yes, please," I whispered.

Chapter Four

Laurence lowered his neck for me to slide down to the ground. "Have a nice time digging," he said kindly.

"I *WILL*!" I blurted in an angry yet tuneful way before wriggling off. I didn't even look around to watch him fly back up to the tree house. Instead, I stuck my head straight in the mud and tunneled down.

It felt like heaven
being in the soft, cool earth again. *This is where I belong,* I thought as I burrowed deeper and deeper. I didn't have to worry about anything when I was underground. But even though I was doing my favorite thing, too many thoughts were popping up in my worm brain. I was worried.

What would I do when I'd finished digging? If I went home, Laurence would still be waiting to visit my auntie's time machine.

I couldn't tell him that it didn't exist. He'd be upset and disappointed that it was all a lie. And then we'd be back at square one, with Laurence doing crosswords and never wanting to leave the house.

If I didn't go home, where would I go? Would I have to stay underground forever? The thought made me shudder. I'd really miss Laurence and the birdhouse *and* that jar of unopened gherkins that needed to be eaten.

I lay down and moaned loudly, "Why can't I be as smart as Albert Einstein? I wouldn't have *any* problems then."

Why?

I felt truly sorry for myself for having such a small worm brain. Hoping it might make me feel better, I started to dig a great big worm tunnel.

When I'd finished, I was very surprised to
see that I'd accidentally made
something quite spectacular.

It was the best tunnel I'd ever dug.
"Ha! I bet Albert Einstein couldn't have
done that!" I chuckled out loud to myself. *And
I bet he couldn't have made something like this . . .*

Perspiring, I stopped to look at what I'd made. It was possibly the most enormous worm tunnel that had ever been dug by a single worm. I'd never seen anything like it, not even in the *Guinness Book of Worm Records*. A warm glow of pride ran through me.

"I think I might be an actual genius — a worm-tunneling genius!" I marveled out loud.

I stopped to take in the greatness of what I had just achieved. It felt amazing being exceptionally good at something. And then I remembered that there are a lot of things I am good at. I paused to make a list in my mind . . .

ALL THE THINGS I'M REALLY GOOD AT:

- Digging tunnels
- Wriggling
- Knowing the answers to Laurence's crossword puzzles
- ~~Lying~~ Making up imaginative stories
- Doing math in my head
- Pretending to be a baguette
- Not being eaten by a bird for breakfast
- Gherkins (eating them)
- Sort of flying to Kenya
- Beatboxing
- Going to the bathroom
- Sometimes having interesting dreams
- Sitting on a chair
- Talking
- Not talking
- Looking out the window

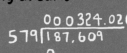

```
          0 0 0 3 2 4. 0 2
   579 | 187, 609
        - 0
         18
        - 0
         187
```

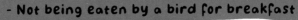

My worm body tingled. Perhaps I was even smarter than Albert Einstein. Why hadn't I noticed before? Why hadn't anyone else noticed? I felt like I had been reborn. Everything seemed different, more straightforward somehow.

I laughed at how the *old me* had struggled to understand quantum physics. Now that I knew I was a genius, I would go back and study that book again. It would be easy. I'd make the time machine, and I'd probably even have time to sew myself a beautiful quilt as well.

I sighed with happiness and started to tunnel back up to the surface. When I popped my head up above the soil, I was surprised to see that instead of being surrounded by the familiar trees next to the birdhouse, I was in the middle of a circle of unfriendly-looking bird beaks.

Perhaps I wasn't so smart, after all. Clearly I had taken a very wrong turn.

Chapter Five

Not this again, I thought as I dangled from the beak of a bird.

He flung me up in the air. I had to think quickly. The only thing that might save me from being eaten was if I did the same thing I'd done when I first met Laurence and tried to engage him in a friendly conversation.

DO YOU HAVE ANY BROTHERS OR SISTERS? DO YOU PREFER DOGS OR CATS? WOULD YOU RATHER BE ABLE TO SNEEZE PICKLED ONIONS OR CRY MILK CHOCOLATE TEARS?

But the bird wasn't interested in talking. Instead, he positioned himself to catch me and swallow me up.

This is it, I thought. I tensed my worm body and closed my eyes tightly as I plunged toward his wide-open beak.

39

Just then I heard a vaguely familiar voice calling out, "Hold on, Bernard. Isn't that Marcus?"

It was too late: I'd landed.

I wasn't sure if I was still alive. I opened one eye and then the other, half expecting to be surrounded by angels in worm heaven. There were no angels, but there were the same birds who had been there two seconds earlier. I glanced up and saw that I was nestled in the wings of Bernard. I knew Bernard. He was one of Laurence's neighbors. Instead of eating me, he'd caught me.

"Are you all right?" he asked. "I didn't realize it was you! You were going to be my midmorning snack."

"I'm fine, thank you," I said, relieved. It was reassuring to see him and other familiar faces.

"How *are* you and Laurence?" Shakira, another of Laurence's neighbors, asked. "We were just saying the other day how we haven't seen you two out and about in forever."

My worm body tensed up again. I didn't want
to tell her about all the problems I was having
with Laurence. I'd have to explain how we stayed
at home all the time doing boring crosswords
and that he hadn't been bothering to take baths
and how annoyed I'd been with him because he
whistled when he breathed and I'd lied about my
auntie having a time machine and I'd left in a huff
because I didn't understand quantum physics and
I thought I might have been a genius but really I
wasn't and I didn't know what I was going to do.

I didn't say anything.

Shakira looked worried. "Has something happened to Laurence?"

She wasn't getting the hint that I didn't want to talk, so I tried changing the subject and said, "Is that the time?" while looking at an imaginary watch on my imaginary wrist.

Shakira looked very worried now and was clutching her wings to her face. "We haven't seen Laurence for weeks, and now you're acting strangely. My bird instincts are telling me something terrible has happened to him."

I didn't want to disappoint her bird instincts, so I made something up. "Well, since you ask," I sighed, "a few weeks ago, Laurence was flying around the woods and he bumped his head on a branch and fell all the way to the ground."

It wasn't a very interesting story, but everyone seemed gripped, and they all gasped at the same time in horror.

"Is he all right?" Shakira asked.

"You know what he's like; he doesn't complain." I was enjoying having everyone's attention and added more details to the story. "He's been at home in bed with a bump on his head. I've been looking after him day and night, reading him stories and making him soup."

"Oh, no. Poor, poor Laurence," Shakira said.

43

Bernard gave me a tight hug before putting me on the ground. "You're such a good friend, looking after him like that. And to think I almost ate you — Laurence's selfless and kindhearted worm friend," he said remorsefully, giving his chest a gentle thump.

A little part of me felt guilty about lying, but the other part felt wonderful that the birds believed my story and thought that I was Laurence's kind and selfless friend.

"Is there anything we can do to help?" Bernard asked. "Should we visit him? Bring him food? Serenade him?"

"He just needs to rest at home and to be left alone," I said quickly, not wanting them to visit and see that he was perfectly fine. "He's much better than he was, and the bump is getting smaller."

"Let us know if there's anything we can do," Shakira said. All of the birds were looking at me with their huge kind eyes. An unexpected thought came to me; maybe they *could* help. . . .

"There *is* one thing that would definitely make things better."

"What is it?" Bernard asked.

The birds gathered in closer. "We'll do anything for him," one of the birds said tunefully.

"I don't know if you'll be able to do it; it's asking a lot. . . ."

"Tell us what it is!" Shakira said.

"Well, ever since Laurence banged his head, he's been having some very strange thoughts. I don't know *where* he got this ridiculous idea from, but he seems to think that my auntie has built a time machine."

"A time machine?"

"Yes, that bonk on the head must have affected his brain a *lot.* This 'time machine' is all he ever talks about, and he'd do anything to see it. I can't bring myself to tell him that it doesn't actually exist."

"How can *we* help?" one of the birds asked cautiously.

"Well," I said casually, "if you could just find a way to build a working time machine and let him give it a try, I'm pretty sure he'd be very happy."

The group took a step back in surprise. A few birds began muttering.

"But that's impossible!"

"We can't do that."

"Time travel hasn't even been invented!"

"This is absolutely ludicrous."

It wasn't long before everyone was moaning and groaning. Then someone piped up with a firm "HUSH!" from the back of the group.

47

Everyone fell silent and made room for the bird to hop forward. "Just what are you all thinking?! You're talking about a bird who you say is your friend, who at this very moment is home in bed with a head injury. It's a disgrace how you are all saying that it's impossible. Helping Laurence to travel in a time machine is the *very* least we can do."

"But *how* can we do it, Vera?" Bernard whispered.

Vera ignored him and looked at me with determined eyes. "*Nothing* is impossible. I've got this, Marcus." She put her wing on her heart and held it there.

I gazed at her in awe. "Do you think you could manage it by the time it stops raining?" I asked softly.

"Yes," she replied in an even softer voice, and then she pivoted on one foot and hopped away with her wings outstretched. "Laurence's dreams are about to come true!" she cried dramatically.

No one said anything. I had worm goose bumps. Maybe Vera was some kind of magical time-traveling bird wizard. I didn't know who or what she was, but I really wanted to believe her.

"Can I give you a ride back to your house, Marcus?" Shakira whispered.

"Yes, please," I said, grateful for the offer, as I wasn't sure where I was.

Everything was working out beautifully. I was getting a ride home, and Vera was going to sort out all my problems.

Nothing could go wrong.

Chapter Six

"Sorry I left in such a huff," I said to Laurence when he opened the front door.

He picked me up and gave me a hug. "It's good to see you, my friend. It was too quiet here without you."

I was glad to be home. The grandfather clock was *ticktock*ing, the smell of baking was wafting from the oven, and Laurence had lots of lumpy crumbs in his feathers.

"Have you been eating cookies?" I asked, nibbling on a morsel.

"A whole box," he admitted, putting me on the floor and then patting himself down. "I'll do some jumping jacks later. How was your digging?"

"It was really good." I wanted to tell him that Bernard almost ate me by accident, but I decided not to. If I told him that, I'd have to tell him about Shakira and how I'd made up a story about him bumping into a branch and getting a mind-altering blow to the head. I was beginning to lose track of the lies I'd told that day, and the guilty feeling was rising in me again. I imagined swallowing it down so that it would go away.

"Would you like some hot chocolate and a slice of homemade cheese-and-leek pie?" asked Laurence.

"There's nothing I'd like more," I replied enthusiastically. I hoped the cheese-and-leek pie would make my guilty feelings go away. "Some gherkins would be nice, too," I added, thinking that might help as well.

"I'll bring the jar!" Laurence said happily, hopping to the cupboard.

We had a cozy night in that evening, eating pie and doing crosswords together. Laurence did lots of jumping jacks and I accidentally ate the whole jar of gherkins. I also did that puzzle, the one with the dog carrying a basket of kittens and flowers.

54

 After almost being eaten that day, it didn't seem so bad staying at home in the warm, dry, cozy birdhouse with Laurence. It was certainly a lot safer. I wondered why I'd been so eager to go out before. A part of me thought Laurence probably had the right idea about staying home all the time. Why go out when everything you need is right here?

I decided that first thing in the morning, I would explain to Laurence that there wasn't really a time machine. I'd made it up. Then we could stay at home every day for the rest of our lives. He'd definitely understand.

That night I listened to the *pitter-patter* of gentle rain on the birdhouse roof as I fell asleep. Apart from having a stomachache from eating too many gherkins, everything was perfect.

Chapter Seven

The sun filtered through the curtains of the bedroom window, gently waking me from a dream about a gherkin that was singing a sad song about a kitten. I did a satisfying waking-up stretch and yawn and then caught a whiff of a heavenly aroma wafting from the kitchen.

Hurrah! It must be Saturday. I smell pancakes! I thought to myself. Laurence always made blueberry pancakes on weekends as a special treat.

"Guess what day it is today?!" he announced as he burst through the bedroom door.

"It's blueberry-pancake day!" I said in a singsong voice.

"It is! And also"—he hopped onto his bed and whipped open the curtains—"it's the day we travel in your auntie's time machine! Look, it stopped raining!"

SWOOSH

SWOOSH

The warm, bright, horrible sunshine flooded every inch of the room, hurting my eyes.

I had to tell Laurence the truth before he got his hopes up too much.

"I CAN'T WAIT! I CAN'T WAIT!" he squealed as he bounced up and down on the bed.

Too late. Laurence was already too excited. I definitely didn't want to tell him now; he'd be really disappointed, and it would all be my fault. I had to think of a way to let him down gently.

"Let's go right after breakfast!" he exclaimed, clapping his wings together.

My head hurt from worrying about what to do. I didn't want to tell Laurence *another* lie.

"I don't feel very well," I said. This wasn't *exactly* a lie because my head actually *was* aching. "I'm not sure if I can go out today, or tomorrow, or ever."

61

"What's wrong?" Laurence asked, looking both worried and disappointed at the same time. He rested his wing on my forehead to check my temperature.

"I've got a sore throat," I croaked in my scratchiest voice. This *was* a lie, but a headache didn't quite sound sick enough.

"Oh, NO!" he said. "You sound *terrible.*" He
tilted his head to one side. "It's strange — you
sounded fine a minute ago when you were looking
forward to your pancakes."

"I know — it came on *so* quickly. You'd better
go without me." I sighed, knowing full well that he
was far too kind to leave me on my own.

"I couldn't possibly leave you on your own," he protested, putting his wing to his breast. "I'll make you a honey and lemon drink and look after you until you get better."

He hopped into the kitchen. I could hear him putting the kettle on the stove and cleaning the frying pan. I mostly felt relieved that we wouldn't be going, but I was also experiencing that pesky guilty sensation again. I swallowed it down so that I wouldn't need to think about it. Funnily, doing that made me feel like I actually did have a sore throat.

"Ooh! What's this?" Laurence was squealing again. He hurried back to the bedroom. "This was under the front door," he said, waving a blue envelope in my face. "It's a letter! The first letter I've *ever* received."

"Who's it from?" I asked curiously as he ripped
it open.

"I don't know. It looks like some kind of
invitation."

"Read it out loud," I said, remembering just in
time to make my voice
all raspy.

Laurence didn't say anything; his eyes were wide.

"What is it?"

"Nothing," he said, stuffing the card back into the envelope. "Drink your honey and lemon."

"Is it something horrible?" I asked.

"No. It's something amazing, but . . . it doesn't matter. Let's just get you feeling better again."

"Tell me what it is!"

He looked at me. "I think it's from your auntie." Laurence took the card out of the envelope again and slowly read it aloud.

Laurence and Marcus are cordially invited to view the only TIME MACHINE in the world. Enclosed are two round-trip tickets for one journey.

Only valid today.

Meet the Keeper of the Key at 10 a.m. at the secret location.

P.S. Marcus knows where the secret location is. (It's where we were yesterday.)

Vera had actually gone and done it! She'd magicked up a time machine with her amazing powers of wizardry. I had butterflies and rainbows dancing in my belly!

"We're going to see the time machine!" I cheered.

"But we *can't*," Laurence said firmly. "You've got a sore throat."

I'd forgotten about that. I cleared my throat. "I feel better now! It's gone away again!" I said, throwing the covers off my bed. "We'd better get going; we don't want to be late."

"Are you sure?"

"Yes, that honey and lemon really did the trick." I gave a little cough. "See! That was the last of it! It's all gone. Let's eat our breakfast. Come on!"

Laurence punched the air and bounced on the bed a few more times.

We ate our pancakes so quickly that we didn't even remember to enjoy them. And in our haste, we left all the dishes in the sink and the beds unmade.

We both went to the bathroom, and just as Laurence was about to open the front door, he said that he felt weird going out without making his bed. So we went back, made the beds, and washed, dried, and put away the dishes. Laurence did some light dusting, then vacuumed the house. We went to the bathroom again, and then we were ready to leave.

Neither of us knew what to expect next.

Chapter Eight

Down a little.

It had been forever since I'd flown with Laurence. I'd forgotten how cozy it was snuggled in his soft feathers. We soared freely above silent treetops in the gentle breeze. The only sound to be heard was my voice calling out the directions. It was blissful to be flying again.

Now loop the loop.

As we approached the secret location, Laurence let out a shrill cry. "THERE SHE IS! THERE SHE IS! I THINK I CAN SEE YOUR AUNTIE!" He made a quick nosedive with a clumsy running landing, narrowly missing a bird on the ground.

My heart skipped a beat with excitement and relief to see that the bird was Vera.

Stay still.

What?

Fly backward

She composed herself hastily and smiled serenely. "Greetings," she said softly. "You must be Laurence and you must be Marcus." She was acting as if she didn't know me. I tried to follow her lead.

"I have no idea who you are; we've definitely never met before."

"I am Vera, Keeper of the Key." She pulled out a key on a large ring from her feathers.

Laurence held his feathery wing tips to his cheeks. "Is that for the time machine?" he asked.

She nodded solemnly. "Yes. Today you shall both embark on a genuine time-traveling adventure." She dangled the key hypnotically in front of Laurence's beak. "Have you brought your invitation?"

"Yes," Laurence replied slowly, following the swinging key with his gaze.

Vera stared fixedly at both of us and then bent down toward some long branches lying on the ground. As she swept them to one side, a great big hole was revealed. It took me a moment to realize that it was the massive worm tunnel I had dug yesterday.

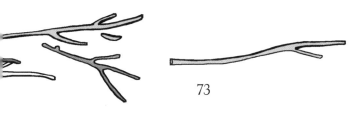

"What's that?" Laurence asked, wrinkling his face in puzzlement.

"*This,*" she announced grandly, "is a wormhole."

Laurence looked less than impressed.

"A *wormhole*?"

"Indeed," Vera explained. "But it's no ordinary wormhole. It's not for worms; it's for time traveling. It's the only existing time-traveling portal on this planet. The time machine is down there."

Vera shone her flashlight into my fantastic wormhole.

"WOW!" Laurence gasped with excitement.

"Shhh." Vera put her wing fingers to her beak. "No one except me — and now you — knows that any of this exists. It must ALWAYS remain a secret."

Laurence was jumping up and down now and trying unsuccessfully to be quiet as he giggled uncontrollably. I couldn't quite believe what was happening. Without even trying, it seemed I'd made an actual time-traveling portal. Perhaps I was a genius, after all. I was excited . . . but also a little bit scared.

"We must go in before anyone sees us," Vera ordered, glancing around.

75

She climbed down a ladder, and we followed. I noticed that Laurence didn't seem to mind getting mud on his feathers like he usually did.

Deep inside the wormhole, Vera flipped a switch, and a dim light revealed a very large and impressive-looking machine. It had clunky switches, levers, and shiny metal pipes.

"Behold the time machine!" she proclaimed proudly.

"It's beautiful," Laurence said with awe, stroking the machine with his wing.

"DON'T TOUCH IT!" Vera asserted in a bold voice.

Laurence quickly whisked his wing away as if he'd touched a piping hot apple pie.

"It's important that you don't touch *anything.*"

Laurence apologized. I was half scared and half full of admiration for Vera. I wanted to touch a lever so that she'd yell at *me,* too. But before I had a chance, Vera ushered us toward two seats at the front of the machine.

"Buckle up," she ordered. "We're almost ready
for takeoff."

"Where are we going?" Laurence asked with a
big goofy smile on his face.

Vera shone the flashlight under her beak
so that we could see her clearly. It was very
dramatic. "You'll be going back in time hundreds
of years."

"This is amazing!" Laurence whispered loudly
to me.

I nodded. "It really is."

We heard a key being turned and a mechanical clunk as a dial was rotated.

"Something's happening," Laurence said, shifting in his seat.

"The machine is powering up!" Vera called from behind us.

Things began to shake and rattle. It felt kind of like someone behind us was jiggling the machine backward and forward. Laurence and I were confused.

Then we heard a *whirring* noise.

WHHHIIIRRR budda budda budda whhhiiirrr . . .
It sort of sounded like a machine, but it also
sounded a lot like Vera just going *"whhhiiirrr*
budda budda."

"This doesn't seem right," Laurence hissed.

"No," I agreed. I was beginning to wonder
whether Vera's time machine actually worked.

A bright beam flashed around the room. It
looked very much like Vera's flashlight.

"What's that, Vera?" Laurence asked.

"It's SCIENCE, Laurence. We are now traveling faster than the speed of light. We're hurtling back through minutes, hours, days, weeks, years, decades, and centuries!"

"Are we?" Laurence asked quietly. "It doesn't even feel like we're moving."

The flashlight-like beam disappeared, and the machine started shaking again. Then we heard *Bing bing bing . . . Bing bing bing!*

"And . . . *Bing!* We've arrived!" Vera announced.

"Do you think this might be a practical joke?" Laurence asked me softly.

"I'm not sure," I answered honestly. Right now, I was as clueless as he was.

We unbuckled ourselves, hopped down from our seats, and went to the back of the machine to meet Vera.

"Prepare yourselves for what happens next," she said in a serious voice. "We've traveled back many centuries, and things may look and feel unfamiliar."

"Excuse me," Laurence said politely with one wing finger raised, "but I don't think we've gone anywhere." He folded his wings.

I nodded in agreement.

"Laurence, Marcus," Vera said patiently, "the science of time travel is *extremely* advanced, and THIS machine has been designed to feel as smooth as possible. If you had experienced the full throttle of the speed at which we were traveling, well, all of your feathers would have fallen out, Laurence. And Marcus, you would have shrunk to the size of a grain of rice."

"Oh, no!" we both replied in unison.

Laurence hugged himself. "Have we really traveled back in time, then?" he asked.

"Yes."

"Really, *really*?"

"Yes. Yes, we have."

"Gosh," he said.

I still wasn't sure whether to believe her, but I didn't like the idea of being turned into a grain of rice.

Light was streaming into the wormhole from the forest. We climbed back up the ladder and found ourselves in a woodland clearing. It looked exactly like the clearing we'd landed in only a few minutes before.

Laurence gazed up at the trees.

"So, are we in the past now?" he asked.

"You are, indeed. We've traveled back in time approximately eight hundred years."

"Oh, my!" he exclaimed. "LOOK! There's a tree, a *really* old tree!" He hopped to it and gave it a hug. "You're an old tree!"

"It looks the same as a modern tree, though," I said to Vera.

She stared deeply into my eyes and said in a kind yet pressing voice, "Trees have not really changed through the passage of time."

I felt funny inside. There was something wonderful about Vera. I wanted to follow her around and listen to everything she said and write songs about her.

She clapped her wings together. "Go and explore the woods. I'll wait here. Make sure you come back to the wormhole when you want to return home."

Laurence was ecstatic and hopped in a tight circle, flapping his wings. "This is amazing, Marcus! I can't believe we've gone back in time!"

He paused for a moment. "Let's explore the forest! We might see even more old trees!" And off he bounced rapidly out of the glade. I had to wriggle as fast as I could to keep up with him.

Laurence picked me up and swung me onto his back.

I had no idea what was really happening, but it was the happiest I'd seen Laurence in a long time, and that made *me* happy.

It was at that moment that we both saw a bird land on a branch. She was wearing very old-fashioned clothing, the kind that might have been worn eight hundred years ago.

I had the shivers.

It *really* was real.

We *had* traveled back in time.

Chapter Nine

"Did you see that medieval bird?" Laurence asked, hopping from one foot to another.

"I did! Let's try to find another one!" My cheeks were beginning to hurt from smiling so much.

"Maybe we'll find a deer!" he said, attempting to keep his voice low.

My eyes darted all around as we hopped toward a dense crop of trees. I wanted to be the first to spot another woodland creature from the past.

"Shhh," Laurence whispered, stopping in his tracks.

"What?"

"Did you hear that noise?"

I stopped to listen. "It sounds like the cars on the highway near our house."

"That's what I thought, too."

"Did they have highways back then?" I asked in a hushed tone.

"No. I don't think they had cars, either." He shrugged. "It must be something else. Probably a babbling brook or a waterfall."

Without warning a bushy-tailed figure suddenly somersaulted into our path.

"AAARGGHHH!" Laurence and I screamed.

It was a squirrel dressed in a nice woolen tunic. "Begging your pardon, I did not mean to startle you," she said.

"It's a medieval squirrel," Laurence whispered discreetly out of the side of his beak.

"She looks like our friend J-Peg from home," I replied softly, copying his talking-out-of-the-side-of-the-mouth technique.

"Yes, she's got the same funny teeth."

"Maybe it's one of her ancestors."

"Why are you talking like that?" the squirrel asked. "I *can* hear you."

"Sorry, we didn't mean to be rude," Laurence mumbled, looking at his feet.

The squirrel didn't seem to mind too much and circled us with cartwheels. "Tell me, mysterious strangers, where have you come from?"

"We're from the future," Laurence announced proudly.

"The future?" she inquired, cartwheeling again. "I think you jest with me." She executed an impressive backflip that left her dangling upside down from a nearby branch.

"It's true," Laurence replied, taking a little hop to the right in an effort to imitate her energetic leaping.

"If you have traveled from the future, then you must be *very* hungry after such a long journey." She somersaulted back to the ground, landing squarely on her feet.

"I am a little hungry, now that you mention it," Laurence admitted sheepishly.

Laurence was always a little hungry.

"In these woods, at this point in history, it is customary to *feed* hungry strangers." She laughed, before jauntily leaning against a tree. "And it just so happens that we have a special banquet prepared!"

"Really?" Laurence asked with a look of delighted disbelief.

"Yes! Follow me and we can eat and celebrate your arrival!" She sprang ahead of us, heading deeper into the forest.

"Ha ha! Okeydokey! We'll be there in a minute!" Laurence called out loudly in a jolly voice. He turned to me. "I don't think we should go," he said seriously.

"We can't *not* go, Laurence. You just said we'll be there in a minute."

"I think it's a trick. I've read about that kind of thing in my Robin Hood book."

Baffled, I stared at him. "What?"

"Robin Hood and his Merry Men would invite strangers to a banquet, but then rob them. They were bandits."

"I thought Robin Hood was supposed to be a good guy."

"He was."

"Robbing people doesn't sound very good or merry," I argued. I looked at the squirrel as she watched us from a distance, scratching her forearms nervously. I wondered if she might actually *be* Robin Hood. To my surprise, when Laurence wasn't looking, she suddenly winked at me.

Why did she do that? Was it some kind of medieval signal to say she was indeed Robin Hood? Or was it to say "Get a move on — your lunch is getting cold"?

"I think she probably *is* a bandit, Laurence. Should we go home?" I suggested. "We've had fun time traveling. We saw all of those old trees and that medieval bird. That's probably enough of an adventure for one day."

"Hmm . . ." Laurence was thinking out loud. "But what if they *are* just being nice? I don't want to miss the chance to eat."

The squirrel seemed to realize that we weren't sure.

We didn't know you were coming, by the way. We always have a big lunch. Also, we're not bandits so you don't need to worry.

"Phew! That puts my mind at ease," Laurence sighed.

"I'm still not sure . . ."

But Laurence had stopped listening and was taking huge bites from a cheese sandwich that he'd pulled out from his feathers.

"What are you doing?"

"Just in case she *is* a bandit, I don't want her getting her paws on my sandwich," he babbled with his mouth full.

"Come on, you two; everyone's waiting!" the squirrel shouted.

"We're coming!" Laurence cried, hopping toward her. I had no choice but to go with him, since I was still on his back.

We can go back to the time machine if we need to, I thought to myself.

We followed a path through the woods that twisted and turned and led us to a truly magical scene. Standing by a tree, beautifully dressed woodland creatures greeted us with warm smiles while a robin sang and played a melodic tune on her lute. Lanterns and flags hung from the branches, and in the fresh forest air there was an aroma of delicious home-cooked food.

"Is that spaghetti Bolognese?" Laurence asked between sniffs.

"It is. Come and have a seat," the squirrel said, leading us to a table full of wooden bowls and silver platters overflowing with quiches, cheese sandwiches, broccoli, toast, fish sticks, apples, black bean burgers, cinnamon zucchini muffins, gherkins, and much, much more.

Laurence's beak fell wide open in disbelief.

"But, these are all my favorite foods! I had no idea they ate this stuff in the olden days. This is like an amazing dream come true!"

It was the biggest feast either of us had ever seen.

"I wish I hadn't eaten that sandwich now,"

Laurence whispered.

Chapter Ten

As we sat at the fancy banquet table, a bird with a puffed-out chest stood behind us, refilling our plates every time we ate something. A crow was playing a flute as the woodland folk tunefully warbled and danced in circles.

"I can't believe this is happening," Laurence mumbled through a beakful of chips. "I don't usually like parties, but this one is really good. It feels like we're in one of my history books."

I couldn't believe it, either. Everything was working out perfectly, and all because of a few huge lies that I'd told Laurence and some birds. I'd always thought telling lies was supposed to be a bad thing, but look at how everything had turned out. We'd actually traveled in a time machine, Laurence and I were feasting like kings, and everyone was having a fantastic time. I felt very proud of myself.

The serving bird put a slice of moist-looking banana cake on my plate. I closed my eyes and opened my mouth, ready to let it melt on my tongue. Instead of being soft and sweet, however, it was hard, cold, and lumpy.

"Ewww!" I spat it out. "What *was* that? It tastes like vinegar!"

Laurence looked at the green lump on my plate. "I think it's a gherkin," he said. "You should try this — it's delicious."

Laurence was eating banana cake.

"Did you just pull a switcheroo?" I asked angrily.

"I'm not sure. What's a *switcheroo*?"

"It's when someone secretly swaps things around and puts a gherkin on your plate when you were expecting a piece of banana cake."

"Yes, I did. I thought you liked gherkins; you're always talking about them."

"I love gherkins, but not when they should be banana cake."

A worm who looked a little like my cousin Gavin interrupted our discussion to offer us some orange juice. As he filled my chalice, he winked at me.

Why was everyone winking at me? Did everyone wink at each other in the olden days? Or did they all need glasses? I was just about to ask Laurence if not wearing glasses made people wink, when the squirrel stood up on a chair. She clanged a gong to attract everyone's attention.

"As you all know, we are celebrating the arrival of two very special guests, Laurence and Marcus, who have traveled here from the distant future."

Gdoing

The small crowd clapped and cheered. A
caterpillar tooted a medieval trumpet.

"To honor and welcome them, we have made a
special pie."

"They're very well organized, aren't they? It's
almost as if they knew we were coming," Laurence
whispered to me as a group paarp
of sparrows wheeled out a gigantic pie.

I was getting a funny feeling in my tummy.
Something wasn't right. How did the squirrel
know our names? And why did everyone look so
familiar?

"Ooh! Look at that!" Laurence cheered. "Is it a
special medieval pie? It's got claws coming out the
sides."

"It's Mole!" screeched a bird who looked just like Laurence's friend Shakira in a piercing whisper. "He's not supposed to be here!"

Laurence and I both knew a mole from back home. He'd tried to cook us in a stew once.

My worm heart began beating more quickly as I glanced around at all of the woodland folk. I recognized every single one of them.

They *weren't* ancestors! They were our actual friends and neighbors. The squirrel was J-Peg, the worm that looked like my cousin Gavin *was* my cousin Gavin. Shakira and Bernard were there, along with ALL of our woodland neighbors, dressed up in medieval costumes.

We hadn't time traveled, after all.

← Tanya

Vera must have somehow organized everything. But I didn't have time to think about how I admired her even more now, because the mole in the pie was noisily clawing his way out.

I had to act quickly. If Laurence recognized him—or any of our neighbors—he would realize that I'd lied about *everything*.

Geoff

Sebastian

Chapter Eleven

The mole had burst his way out of the pie. There was a crusty mess all over the ground.

"Surprise! It's ME, Mole! You forgot to invite me to the party!"

Everyone looked horrified except for
Laurence, who was clapping wildly
and cheering with delight. "This is
AMAZING! It's so much fun in medieval times!"

As Mole brushed his fur with
his claws to get rid of the pie
crumbs, Laurence studied
Mole's face. He turned
to me and whispered
through a giggle,

"He looks just like

that horrible mole

who tried to eat us!"

"He's probably a very distant
relative," I babbled quickly.

"WHY IS EVERYONE STARING AT ME?"
Mole shouted. "Come on, you guys—it's
time to get the party started!"

"Oh, goody! Can we play musical
chairs?" Laurence cried.

"Great idea!" I yelled, hoping that dancing around some chairs might distract Laurence from noticing any more familiar faces. "Everyone, line up the chairs; you there, play us a tune," I said firmly to a pigeon with a violin. He nervously played "Twinkle, Twinkle, Little Star" at top speed, over and over again.

"Don't just stand there, you knuckleheads! Get moving!" Mole barked at everyone.

"Yay!" exclaimed Laurence, immediately hopping joyfully around the chairs. He was giggling. "I love this game!"

No one else wanted to play.

Mole grabbed a cockroach from the crowd. "Come and join in," he ordered. The cockroach did as he was told, skipping miserably to the tune. Mole shoved the creatures one by one toward the row of chairs.

119

"You too, worm," Mole said, looking in my direction. He narrowed his eyes and scrunched up his face. "Don't I *know* you?"

Wanting to hear what Mole was saying, the pigeon stopped playing the violin. Everyone playing musical chairs rushed to claim a chair.

"Aw, we *all* get to sit down. There's supposed to be one missing," Laurence grumbled with disappointment.

"WE'VE DEFINITELY NEVER MET BEFORE, MOLE," I said a little unconvincingly.

"You're lying. I know exactly who you are."
Mole was making his way toward me; he looked
angry. The pigeon started playing "Twinkle,
Twinkle, Little Star" again, this time at twice the
speed. All the animals were frantically running
around the chairs, trying to keep up.

Mole was just about to grab me with his long claws when Laurence shouted out, "Stop being horrible to my friend, you medieval meanie! He's NOT lying; we're from the future!" And, to my amazement, he smashed a huge ripe tomato onto Mole's head.

Everyone stopped what they were doing to watch the mole staggering about.

"What's happening? I can't see anything," Mole warbled angrily from inside the tomato.

"I've got a good idea," Laurence muttered to me.

"What is it?"

"Let's go back to the future before the mole takes the tomato off."

"OK," I agreed. Laurence flung me on his back and began hopping at full speed along the forest path, heading back toward Vera's time machine.

I did think about telling Laurence that we hadn't really time traveled and that the time machine wouldn't be able to help us. But I decided to keep quiet.

Phoo Phoo

"I'm so glad we can get out of here." Laurence laughed with relief. "Otherwise we'd be in big, big troub—"

"You ARE in trouble," boomed a sinister voice. "Big, BIG trouble!"

"Fly, Laurence, fly!" I screamed.

But it was too late. I felt a claw on the back of my neck. . . .

Chapter Twelve

Laurence and I were being punished in a medieval way.

"I wonder if Vera is still waiting for us back at the time machine." Laurence sighed forlornly. "And even if she is, we're not going to be able to go back to the future now, are we?"

"I think we're going to be stuck here for a very long time," I said sadly. "Probably forever."

Laurence didn't say anything for a while.

"At least we're together. There's no one else I'd rather be locked up with. You've been such a good friend, Marcus," he went on. "I still can't believe you let me come with you in your auntie's time machine. If I could put my wing on my heart, I would say that this is the most amazing thing I've *ever* done."

He tried to put his wing on his heart, but couldn't quite reach because of the stocks.

A lump rose in my throat. I felt awful. He thought I'd been a good friend, but if he knew how many lies I'd told him and the others, he'd think differently. I would never be able to tell him the truth now; it would break his heart. Also, he'd definitely be angry with me. It was my fault that we were locked up with no chance of escape. It was best to keep my worm lips firmly sealed.

Just then, I heard footsteps and murmurings coming from the other side of some bushy shrubs.

"Do you think it's that meanie mole returning?" Laurence whispered in a panic. "He might do something even more horrible to us."

"What *is* going on in these woods?" asked a voice behind the shrubs. It didn't sound like Mole.

"I'm too scared to call for help," I whispered to Laurence. "It might be another bad guy."

Laurence and I both strained to hear the conversation.

Another voice piped up. "You must be the only one who hasn't heard. Vera, that bird who runs the forest drama group, has put on a huge production. Tons of woodland folk have gotten involved to create a medieval banquet. Everyone rehearsed all through the night."

"Is that why there are strange objects all over the woods?"

"Yes. Bernard made LOTS of props. They're very realistic. He's got a real talent for it. . . ."

They were saying too much! I couldn't risk Laurence hearing any more.

"It's rude to listen in on other people's conversations," I whispered. "Should we sing a song instead?" I started humming.

Laurence tutted. "Quiet, Marcus! I want to hear what they're saying."

"But why did they do it?" the first voice went on.

"It was for a bird from Oak Tree Woods. I can't remember his name now. Apparently he had a bump to the head and that made him obsessed with the idea of time travel."

"Who are they talking about?" Laurence asked.

"I'm not really interested. I'm too busy singing."

Tum te tummmm

"Was it that little round bird who looks like a chicken?"

"Yes, the one who's friends with a worm. The worm was the one who arranged it with Vera as a present for him. They're a very strange pair."

"Marcus, *stop* it!" Laurence was getting frustrated with my humming.

"HMMMM HMM HMM!"

"I think I know the bird you mean. Is he the one who was convinced he was a flamingo?"

"That's him."

"Ah, yes, I remember now. Laurence. He's completely deluded, that bird, and gullible, too. Fred said he didn't realize it was a play. He actually thought they'd time traveled."

"He didn't? Ha ha ha! What an idiot!"

I didn't dare look at Laurence.

"They're talking about *me,* aren't they, Marcus?" Laurence wailed.

The animals heard Laurence's cry.

"We'd better go," one said before scurrying away.

There was a moment of silence. I gulped.

"What IS going on, Marcus?"

I laughed weakly. "Don't listen to those gossips. They're making up silly stories!"

"But they're not, though, are they?" Laurence asked in a wobbly voice. "We *haven't* time traveled. It was all pretend. Vera made it all up. . . ."

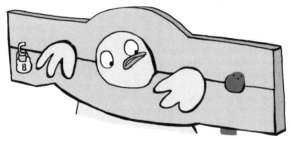

I didn't say anything. My cheeks were burning. I couldn't tell if Laurence was sad or angry; he was probably both.

"Admit it, Marcus," he said loudly. "You lied to me about your auntie inventing a time machine, didn't you?"

I nodded ashamedly. "Yes, it was a lie."

"I KNEW it! And why did you tell everyone that I bumped my head?"

"I didn't want you to be disappointed that there wasn't really a time machine, so I told everyone that a bang on your head made you think my auntie had built a time machine and you really wanted to try it out."

With great effort I turned to look at Laurence. His beak was wide open with shock.

"Vera told me she'd figure it out. I thought she was a magical wizard and so I went along with it. I didn't realize it was a play, either."

Even though he seemed more than a little taken aback, it was a relief to be able to tell Laurence the truth at last. I wished I'd told him sooner! Having such a big secret had felt like I was wearing an invisible coat that was made out of concrete and iron, really heavy and uncomfortable. But now I felt as light and free as a butterfly doing ballet. I was filled with gratitude that he was taking this so well. He was an amazing friend; he was always patient, calm, and understanding.

"I CAN'T believe you lied to me AND everyone in the forest!" he exploded in a not very patient, calm, or understanding way. "Now everyone thinks I'm a fool. They're all laughing at me. How could you DO this to me?"

I tried to explain. "I really didn't mean for it to turn out like this, Laurence. . . ."

"I don't want to hear any more. You're a lying traitor. And now I'm locked up with you in this thing *forever*."

"I'm really, really, really sorry, Laurence, for lying to you. And I'm sorry for hurting you. I wish I could undo this whole mess."

Laurence didn't say anything. He turned his head away from me.

Knowing I'd upset Laurence so much made my heart hurt. I felt like a field plowed by a tractor. There was nothing I could do to stop Laurence from being upset with me. Not even the time machine could help, because it wasn't real.

Birds sang in the distance. An airplane flew

overhead. A couple of large leaves fell noisily from a tree.

"Aren't you going to speak to me anymore?" I squeaked.

"No, because you're a liar, liar, pants on fire."

I switched from feeling like a sad plowed field to feeling very angry.

"Well, Laurence," I burst out, "I only did it because I was sick of watching you sit around on the sofa every single day like a great big lump of mashed potatoes."

"What's that supposed to mean?" he asked, raising his voice.

"You never want to do anything fun anymore."

"Yes, I do! I make sure we do crossword puzzles every single day!"

"I don't WANT to stay at home doing stupid crossword puzzles."

"I thought you LIKED doing them! You always know the answers."

"I just want to go out and have adventures and fun, and for us to enjoy being together like we used to."

"Why didn't you SAY something, then? It would have been much, much easier than getting everyone in the forest involved in your ridiculous stories."

"I DID say something. YOU DIDN'T LISTEN TO ME!" *I* was shouting now.

Laurence was about to shout back when, without warning, an unidentified flying object fell from the sky and landed directly in front of us.

BLOOOMFF-SQUELCH!

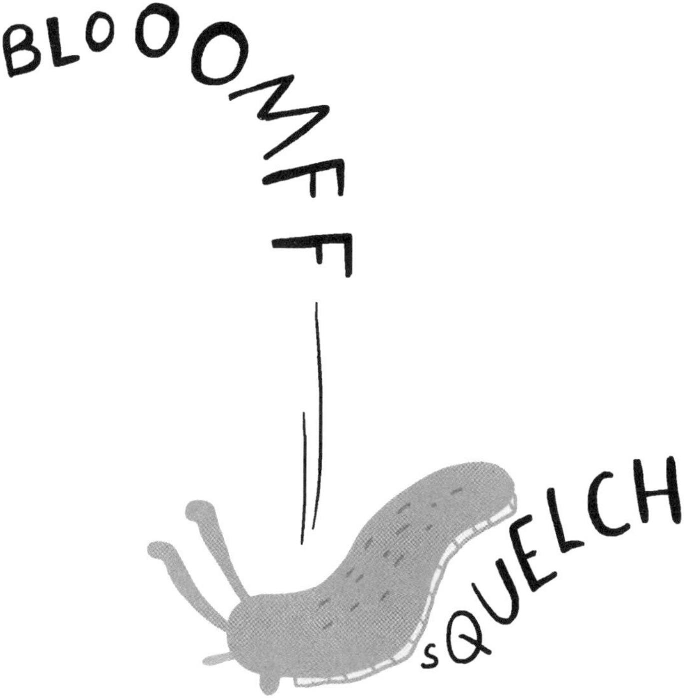

BLOOOMFF

sQUELCH

Neither of us spoke as we studied the gray blob in front of us.

"Is it . . . alive?" Laurence asked, forgetting we were in the middle of a momentous argument.

The blob raised its top end. *"Oooff!"* it whimpered.

"Yes, I think it is."

Chapter
Thirteen

Laurence and I were watching the blob as it
writhed on the ground when . . .

BLOOOMFF-SQUELCH

and then

BLOOOMFF

two more squishy gray things fell from the sky
and landed in the same spot.

"Are they . . . slugs?" Laurence gasped.

"I'm not sure," I replied doubtfully. I didn't think slugs could fly.

The first blob lifted its head. "Is everyone all right?" it mumbled slowly.

"Yes," the others groaned.

"We'd better go and do that again," the first blob said. They all made moany-groany sounds as they flopped over onto their bellies.

"Excuse me, but what kind of creatures are you?" Laurence quizzed politely as they started to crawl slowly away, leaving a slightly disgusting trail of slime behind them.

They stopped and the first blob spoke. "We're slugs."

"Oh, you are? Are you a special *flying* breed?"

The slug spokesperson looked at us with a dazed expression. "We're not special. We didn't fly; we were flung here as part of the Slug Games."

"The Slug Games?" Laurence asked. "What are those?"

I was relieved that this unusual distraction had made him completely forget he was angry with me.

"Yes, tell us everything!" I joined in gratefully.

"I'm still angry with you, Marcus, by the way," he reminded me.

The slug shrugged. "It's something Mole invented."

Laurence shuddered. "*Awful* Mole?"

"Yes, him. He's got a catapult, and for fun, he fires us into the woods. The slug that flies the farthest is the winner."

"Do you enjoy that kind of thing?" Laurence asked.

"No!" they answered together.

"So, why do you do it?"

They looked at Laurence as if he'd asked a very ridiculous question. "Because Mole is bigger than us. And he's scary."

"Oh! He's such a bully!" I piped up. "If I wasn't locked up in these stocks, I'd hit him on the head with his silly catapult."

"Yes!" Laurence agreed. "And I'd pick him up by his tiny little mole ears and send *HIM* flying!"

"Why?" the first slug asked slowly.

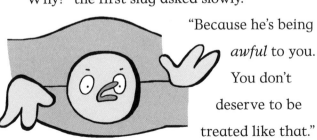

"Because he's being *awful* to you. You don't deserve to be treated like that."

They looked at one another. "But we're *slugs;* no one likes us," the first slug said.

"You shouldn't be treated badly just because you're slugs."

They were all surprised. "That's the nicest thing anyone has ever said to us," the same slug said.

"It's too bad we're locked up; otherwise we'd definitely help you," Laurence said regretfully.

"Thanks for the kind thought. We'd better get back before Mole comes looking for us."

They began crawling away again. The smallest slug stopped and turned around. "Before we go, do you want us to help *you*?"

"There's nothing you can do. Mole locked us up and threw away the key," Laurence said matter-of-factly.

"Look, it *does* have a lock!" one of the slugs said.

"That Bernard is very smart, isn't he!" The little slug marveled.

Laurence managed to hold the tip of his wing aloft. "What do you mean by that?" he asked.

"They're not real stocks. Bernard made them out of cardboard for Vera's medieval production."

Laurence and I gasped. Laurence gave the stocks a little shake. The slugs were right: they *were* made out of cardboard and were very flimsy.

One of the slugs crawled over and took a bite. The others followed, and Laurence and I watched in amazement as they gnawed away at the contraption. I'm not sure how long we stood there waiting for them to finish eating, but it felt like a very long time.

"Eating cardboard is such a treat!" one
commented with a little smile.

nibble

Groan

Bleugghh

When they'd finished, Laurence picked me up and threw me into the air. "We're free, Marcus!" he cheered.

"Ha ha, we can fly home now!" I cried gleefully. I felt relieved and was even happier that Laurence didn't seem to be upset anymore.

"So, you're free," said a chilling, mocking voice behind us.

It was Mole. He was filing his claws while leaning against a hefty-looking catapult. "Are you going to hit me on the head with this catapult, little worm?" he sneered.

It didn't seem like such a good idea now that Mole was standing in front of me in real life.

"I didn't think so. You two are as pathetic as these slugs."

The slugs were crawling toward Mole for the next round of the Slug Games.

"Should we just fly home?" I whispered eagerly to Laurence.

"No!" Laurence said firmly. "We can't leave these poor creatures with *him*. WE'RE not the ones who are pathetic — YOU are, Mole!" he shouted.

Mole clenched his sharp claws into fists. "What did you say?" he snarled menacingly.

What was Laurence doing? He was picking the wrong creature to stand around and have an argument with.

Chapter Fourteen

"You heard me, Mole. You're a sad, pathetic bully, and no one even likes you. You're only picking on these poor little slugs to make yourself feel better," Laurence stated bravely.

The slugs looked terrified. Part of me wanted Laurence to zip it, but the other part of me wanted to hear more. My friend sounded like some kind of mind doctor who understood the inner workings of a wickedly evil mole.

Mole waddled over to where Laurence and I were standing. I felt an overwhelming urge to burrow into the ground and dig one of my fantastic worm tunnels, but I didn't think now would be a good time to abandon Laurence. Especially as he'd only just gotten over his bad mood with me.

"If you want to play the Slug Games again, we're ready and waiting," a slug called out nervously from the catapult, trying to protect Laurence from Mole's terrible temper.

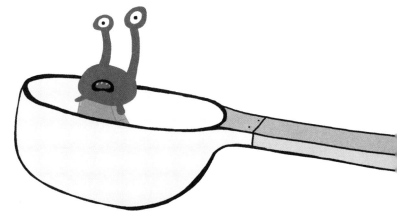

"You don't need to play the Slug Games anymore. You can get down from there," Laurence called out with authority.

The slugs glanced uneasily at one another, unsure whether to do what he said.

"I said," he repeated, "get down from there!"

They quickly crawled back down to the ground and huddled together, trembling.

"So! I'm a bully," Mole whispered menacingly, inches from Laurence's face, "and no one likes me?"

"Mm-hmm," Laurence agreed, and flinched. I couldn't tell if he was frightened or if he was being blasted by Mole's eye-wateringly bad onion breath.

"You're a fine one to talk," Mole seethed. "The only friend you have is a *worm*." He laughed, just like a true bad guy. "What kind of a ridiculous friendship is that? He's not even a real friend. He set you up to make you look like a fool in front of everyone."

"I didn't mean to, Laurence," I began to babble.

"Silence, worm," Mole commanded. He laughed again. "Of course, it wasn't difficult to make you look stupid. Everyone knows how gullible you are." Mole was circling us now like a detective on a TV show. "I need to choose your punishment very carefully. Perhaps I'll fire *you* out of the catapult, too, just like those slugs you pretend to care about."

"Laurence has wings; he can fly away any time he wants to," I said defiantly.

Mole stepped back. "Go on, then — do as your little worm friend says," he said softly, flapping his arms mockingly. "Fly away."

Laurence didn't move. "The slugs can't fly away from you, so neither will I. I'm staying here in support of my non-winged friends."

"See what I mean?" Mole lowered his gaze to stare at me and tapped my forehead with a pointy claw. "Your bird friend doesn't have much going on up here, does he?"

Mole picked up a long piece of ivy from the forest floor and began to tie Laurence's wings behind his back. Laurence didn't even try to stop him. Instead, he closed his eyes and held his head high with an air of mysterious dignity.

"Ha ha! There! You can't fly away *now*," Mole sneered. "You really are just like one of your non-winged friends. Get over there with the slugs, both of you."

"You're right, I'm not very bright," Laurence exclaimed theatrically as Mole marched us over to the catapult. I glanced at him and he gave me a wink. Not another creature winking at me!

"I'm so *stupid* that I don't even know the answers to my own crossword puzzles. I always have to ask Marcus to help me."

I still had no idea what was going on. I was clueless.

"For example, right now I'm stuck on One Down." He winked again. "It's ten letters, and the first letter is *S*."

I got it! Laurence was speaking to me in a secret code! Tingles ran down my back.

"And the clue," he went on, "is *when a banana cake becomes a gherkin*."

Straightaway I knew the answer to Laurence's cryptic clue: *switcheroo*. He was talking about earlier when he swapped my banana cake for a gherkin at the medieval banquet. I knew EXACTLY

what he wanted me to do!

"We don't want to hear about your stupid, boring crossword puzzles. Get in that catapult, all of you!" Mole demanded. "I'm going to fire you so far away, you'll never find your way home!"

"Your silly machine can't do that," I scoffed.

"Yes, it can. Get in."

"It's definitely not strong enough to hold all of us," I argued. "It's just made out of cardboard. It's going to break."

"It IS strong enough and it's NOT made from cardboard," Mole yelled angrily. "I should know: I made it myself!"

I gasped dramatically. "You didn't make *this*. It's *too* good."

Mole tried unsuccessfully to hide a proud smile. "I DID make it. I made it ALL by myself."

"Wow!" I gushed. "It's pretty impressive." I looked the machine up and down and wriggled around it to admire it from every angle. "How does it work exactly?"

By now, the slugs were looking confused and extremely anxious.

Mole became animated, thrilled by my interest.

"Let me show you! First, you put a slug in like this." He lobbed the smallest slug into the bucket and leaped over to a wooden wheel. "Next, you spin this to pull back the load, and then—"

I cocked my head to one side and made an unimpressed face.

"What's wrong?" he asked.

"That slug is too light. I don't believe the bucket can hold a heavier load."

"It CAN."

"Really?" I said in my most disbelieving voice.

"Yes. I'll show you with Laurence." He tossed the poor slug out and picked Laurence up.

I shook my head.

"Still not heavy enough?" he asked with a sigh.

"We need a more solid creature for the demonstration," I argued, looking around for a suitably solid creature.

"I know!" Mole said with excitement. "*I* could get in to show you."

"Hmm. That's not a bad idea," I replied casually.

Mole enthusiastically clambered up into the bucket.

"And then do I spin this wheel?" I asked.

"Yes! And as you can see, that pulls the bucket back like so," Mole called down. "The catapult uses tension, torsion, and gravity to fling a load into the air — it's simple physics!"

The catapult creaked and groaned with the weight of Mole pulled back tight.

"And how do you release the load?" I asked innocently.

"By spinning the wheel the other way. But don't do that *now* or else *I'll* be fired away."

"Fire away, did you say?" I asked, spinning the wheel back the other way.

"What? NOOOOOOO!" Mole screamed.

The bucket sprang back to the upright position, flinging Mole into the air at tremendous speed.

KERRPLUNNNGGGGGGGGGGGG!

We all watched with our mouths and beaks wide open as Mole rocketed high into the sky.

KERRPLUNNNG

"Ha ha! You did it, Marcus!" Laurence roared with laughter as he hopped from one foot to the other. "You pulled the switcheroo!"

"And you used a secret code!" I cheered.

"Will he come back to get us?" one of the slugs asked nervously.

"Not anytime soon," Laurence said reassuringly. "He'll have landed miles away."

"We're free!" I cheered. "We can go home and speak in secret crossword code!"

Laurence scooped me and all of the slugs up in his wings. "Let's ALL go home," he announced. "We can ALL spend the evening talking in secret crossword code."

It felt snuggly and safe in the warm embrace of friendship. Suddenly I remembered the argument we'd been having.

"Laurence," I asked timidly, "are you still angry with me?"

He hugged me tighter. "No," he said. "I don't think you meant to be a nincompoop and hurt my feelings."

"I really didn't. It all just got out of hand."

"And as it turned out, we did have a great adventure traveling back in time, even if it wasn't real."

"It felt real, though. I wish it WAS real. I'd go back and do that all again."

"Me too."

"I don't mean to interrupt," squeaked a little voice from Laurence's left armpit, "but can you put us down, please?" It was one of the slugs.

"Oh! Sorry." Laurence carefully placed the slugs back on the ground.

"Thanks for helping us," they said politely, "and for inviting us over to your house. Maybe we could do that *another* time. We'd really like to go home now."

We said our goodbyes and watched the slugs crawl away, their trails of slime glistening magically in the afternoon sunshine.

"Do you think they *will* come over another time?" I asked.

"Probably not," Laurence said. He sighed with satisfaction and then yawned. "Should we go home and make a vegetable pie?"

"Three letters, beginning with *Y* and ending with *S*," I answered in crossword code. "The clue is *the opposite of no*."

Laurence didn't know what I was talking about. We flew home.

We didn't get around to making our pie that evening. Instead, we talked and talked about everything and only stopped when Laurence fell asleep, beak first, into his mug of hot chocolate. We'd been up all night.

Chapter Fifteen

The next few weeks were a blur.

Vera's medieval banquet play had been so popular that she decided to repeat it every day. Forest creatures came from far and wide to take part and experience *The Secret Time Machine*.

Laurence and I joined Vera's drama club and we even organized our own productions. I staged *The Worm Experience.*

Laurence put on a *Fly Me to the Moon* performance.

For some reason, these weren't as popular as the medieval banquet.

No one has seen Mole since we catapulted him into the sky. Sometimes I wonder if he landed so far away that he had to start a completely new life. I hope he's not so awful these days.

The slugs never did take up Laurence's

invitation to come over to
the house for a speaking-
in-secret-crossword-code
evening. They are too busy
being famous. One of the
slugs wrote a book about
their experience with Mole,
and now they spend their

time giving motivational speeches in schools and
libraries.

They even appeared on a daytime talk show.

Laurence and I have become good friends with Vera. She comes to our house every week and sits on the sofa. Sometimes we don't even say anything; we just look at one another. Other times, Vera will tell us stories about her life or other animals. These stories really make you think.

Even though she isn't a wizard, there is something magical about Vera. She brings out the best in both of us and inspires us to try new things.

Sometimes when Vera comes to the house, she helps us talk and listen to each other about the things that really matter to us.

It makes a big difference and means that we don't get on each other's nerves as much.

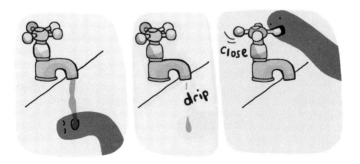

Laurence and I leave the house a lot more these days, and we've started having adventures again, just like we used to. Laurence has also been going out on his own, meeting up with his friends. He'll often go to the zoo with J-Peg, Shakira, and Bernard. I'll go out digging on my own and make elaborate and fancy worm tunnels. One of the fun things about *not* spending time with each other is that when we meet up again, we have lots of new and interesting things to talk about.

Bernard landed on a crocodile by accident!

I saw another worm today!

These days, I hardly notice when Laurence is breathing noisily or making disgusting beak-clearing sounds. Even when he is being annoying, I still really like him. I really, really like Laurence, and before all of this happened I didn't even know it was possible to care about someone this much.

Laurence hasn't touched his crossword puzzle books in a long time. He is too busy doing other things. He read the quilting book and made a beautiful quilt for my auntie.

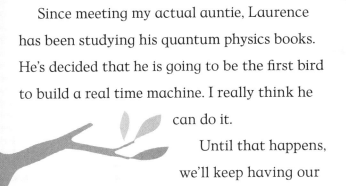

Since meeting my actual auntie, Laurence has been studying his quantum physics books. He's decided that he is going to be the first bird to build a real time machine. I really think he can do it.

Until that happens, we'll keep having our adventures.

Thanks

With special thanks to my husband, Tim, for his amazing kindness, support, and belief in me. Thank you for looking after our little AJ so beautifully while I wrote and drew the pictures for this story.

Thanks to everyone at Walker Books, especially Lizzie, for the adventures we've shared while bringing Marcus and Laurence to life.

Thank you to Grandma, Da, and family, and to Madeleine, Liv, Gabriel, Hilary, Becky, and Evie for your encouragement.

And a squeaky shout-out to Berwyn, Indi, Lois, and Ivy.

About the Author

Award-winning artist and writer Simone Lia began painting and drawing in her dad's toolshed at the age of thirteen, before going on to study at the University of Brighton and then the Royal College of Art. She writes "The Simone Lia Cartoon," a weekly comic strip published in the *Observer*, and has written weekly comics for numerous publications, including the *Independent on Sunday* and the *Phoenix*.

She has written and illustrated several books for children and adults, including *They Didn't Teach THIS in Worm School!*, which was her debut novel, and the graphic novels *Fluffy* and *Please God, Find Me a Husband!*

Simone Lia lives and works in London.